Copyright © 2021 by Semaj Rashad

All rights reserved. No part of this book may be reproduced or used in any manner without written permission of the copyright owner except for the use of quotations in a book review.

Tiny Teal Books
www.tinytealbooks.com
Follow us on social:
@tinytealbooks

Juvenile Fiction / Social Themes / Self-Esteem & Self-Reliance
Juvenile Fiction / Stories in Verse
Juvenile Fiction / Social Themes / New Experience

Book design by April Rashad
Illustrations by Annie Wilkinson

ISBN paperback: 978-1-7364138-0-7
ISBN ebook: 978-1-7364138-1-4

This book is dedicated to the creative
that lives in all of us.

For my wife, April, and my sons Anias and Noah,
you inspire me every day.

Additionally, this book wouldn't be possible without my family, friends, and the dozens of other strangers who supported me in bringing this book to life. I hope that your assistance in fulfilling one of my dreams compels countless others to color the world and color it well in their own way.

"Color the world and color it well,"

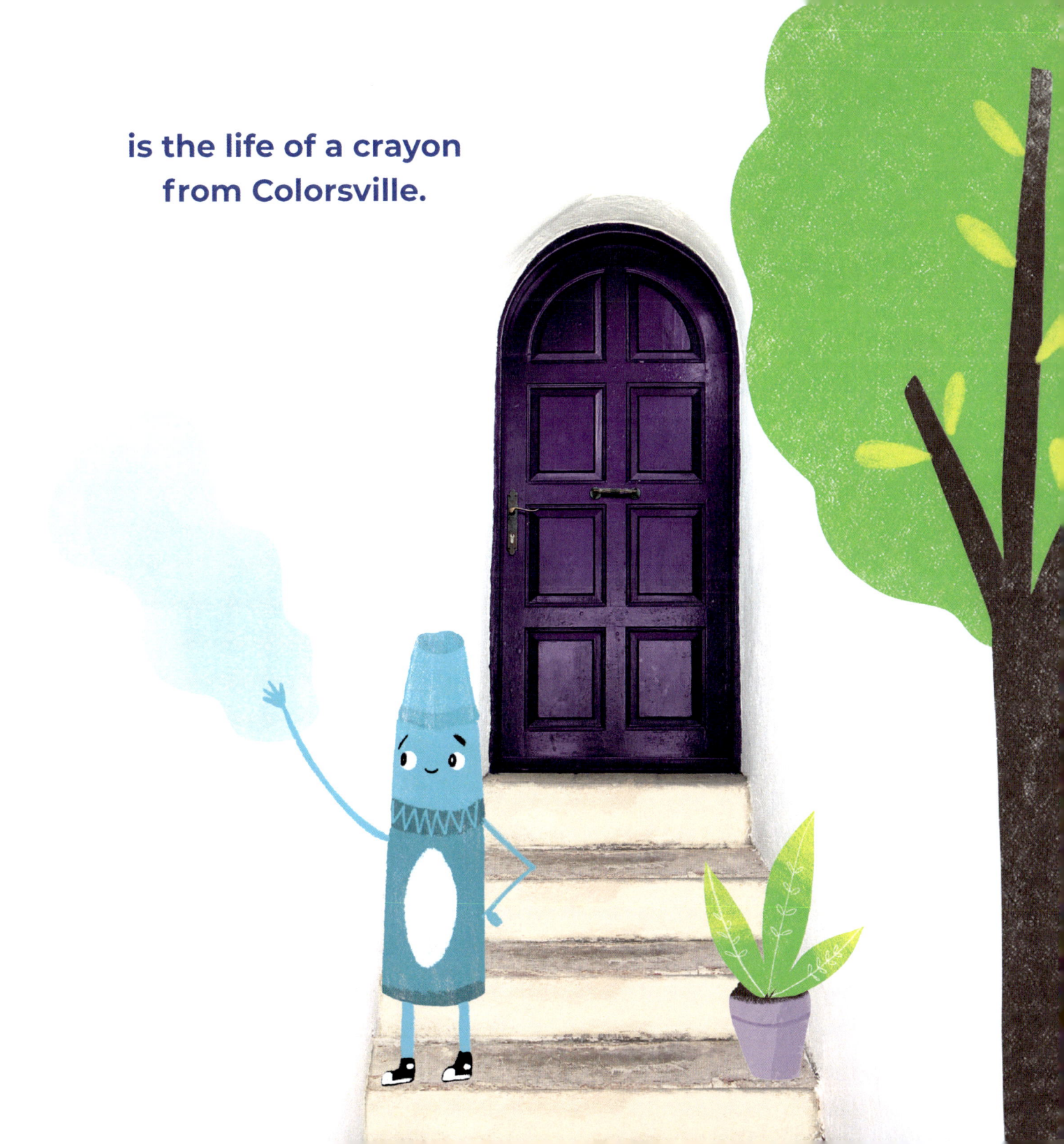

is the life of a crayon from Colorsville.

Green has grass and the leaves of the trees.

Blue has the sky and each of the seas.

But Tiny Teal felt stuck in between.
He wasn't quite blue, and he wasn't quite green.

"Don't be so down," his mom would say.
"You'll find something to color one day."

"It can be hard, and you may be sad.
But keep on trying," said Tiny Teal's dad.

But...Tiny Teal wasn't green, nor was he blue.
He wondered, "what is it my color should do?"

"The sky, the seas, the grass, the trees,
I could never color these."
Nothing fit, his color, his face,
Tiny Teal felt out of place.

So, he made up his mind to do some exploring, because to not color would be awfully boring.

He explored by car
and a rocket to Mars.

What did he find? What did he see?
He found all sorts of things he could be.

Like swimming in the ocean, that was his wish, so he chose to color a school of fish.

He also longed to flutter and fly, so he colored many butterflies.

Although it's one of the coldest sites, he shined up there with the Northern Lights.

Speaking of cold, he thought it nice to sparkle in and through the ice.

**Flowers spinning, rivers flowing,
beetles, peacocks, and gemstones glowing.**

A tiny island with a beach,
an ocean wave, a great big reef,

He shared all his stories and what he had learned.

How he kept searching so high and so low.
And because he never quit, he now knows,

"I'm Tiny Teal. I'm green and blue and I have so much I'm made to do."
Just like you!

Here are some questions, conversation starters and activities that can help you discuss diversity and differences with your family and little ones:

1. After reading this story, what was your favorite part of Tiny Teal's journey? Why?
2. Tiny Teal wanted to find his purpose. Do you think he found it? What do you think it is? What do you think you were made to do?
3. Have you ever felt that you didn't fit in with others? How does that make you feel?
4. Ask your parents and other family members "where do we come from?" Use this question to explore your family's cultural history.

Look for more engaging questions at tinytealbooks.com

Bonus activities:

- **Explore:** Use a map or globe to share the different cities, states, countries and continents your family is from.

- **Experience:** Learn about an upcoming holiday, recipe or tradition from one of the places your family is from.

- **Engage:** Share photos of you and other family members as far back as you can go. Call or video chat a family member who lives in another city, state, country from you.

- **Draw** your favorite part of the story and email us to tinytealbooks@gmail.com or tag us @tinytealbooks on Instagram.

Here are five Bible verses to help your child learn about their God-given purpose:

- "Many are the plans in a person's heart, but it is the LORD's purpose that prevails." – Proverbs 19:21

- "And God is able to bless you abundantly, so that in all things at all times, having all that you need, you will abound in every good work." – 2 Corinthians 9:8

- "Being confident of this, that he who began a good work in you will carry it on to completion until the day of Christ Jesus." – Philippians 1:6

- "Great are your purposes and mighty are your deeds. Your eyes are open to the ways of all mankind; you reward each person according to their conduct and as their deeds deserve." – Jeremiah 32:19

- "Every good and perfect gift is from above, coming down from the Father of the heavenly lights, who does not change like shifting shadows." – James 1:17

Photo Credits:

(Page 4) Town - Freestocks on Unsplash

(Page 5) Door image - Matt Artz on Unsplash

(Page 6) Forest - Mateusz Stępień on Unsplash

(Page 7) Beach - Nour Elhakim on Unsplash

(Page 8) Ant Rozetsky on Unsplash

(Page 9) Angela Pham on Unsplash

(Page 10) Santorini, Greece, George Desipris

(Page 11) Teal Car, Cancún, Mexico, Erik Odiin

(Page 12) Town - Ugur Peker on Unsplash

(Page 13) Greece, Sigmund on Unsplash

(Page 14) Lake - Ian Cylkowski on Unsplash

(Page 15) Gareja Mountain, Georgia, Orlova Maria on Unslash

(Page 16) Madrid, Spain, Paul Lucaci @paulglucaci

(Page 17) Space, Sergey Nivens on Adobestock

(Page 18) Jelly fish - Jack B @nervum on Unsplash

(Page 19) Perhentian Islands, Malaysia, Céline Haeberly on Unsplash

(Page 20) Background - Rodion Kutsaev on Unsplash
Butterflies - Adobestock

(Page 21) Iceland, Benjamin Suter on Unsplash

(Page 22) Diamond Blue Ice Cave near Jökulsárlón, Iceland - Agnieszka Mordaunt

(Page 23) Succulent - Meritt Thomas on Unsplash
Beetle - Egor Kamelev on Pexels
Peacock - Ricardo Frantz on Unsplash
Gems - Judith Zimmermann on Unsplash

(Page 24) Maldivian lagoon, A. Shuau (Obofili) on Unsplash

(Page 25) Hummingbird - Volcano Antisana, Ecuador, Chris Charles on Unsplash
Bird (Bottom right) Hunei District, Hunei, Taiwan, Boris Smokrovic on Unsplash
Duck (right) - Jason Leung on Unsplash
Duck (left)

(Page 26) Mahia, New Zealand, Mathyas Kurmann on Unsplash

(Page 27) Amphitheater Hugo Sousa

(Page 28) Mountain - Umhausen, Paul Gilmore, on Unsplash

(Page 29) Pulpit Rock, Norway, Maksim Shutov on Unsplash

Made in the USA
Middletown, DE
14 April 2022